this book belongs to :

The zizka family

FRANK THE CAT

Frank the Cat

Copyright © 2010 by **Polyester Music Productions**

ISBN 978-0-9864733-0-2

Polyester Music Productions
p.o. box 16168
1199 Lynn Valley Road
North Vancouver, BC
V7J 3S9

Email: www.angelakelman.com
www.singalongbooks.ca

*For my son, Alex, who perpetually fills
my heart with love and laughter.*

AK

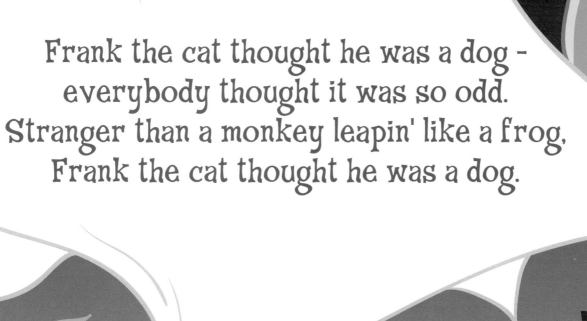

Frank the cat thought he was a dog -
everybody thought it was so odd.
Stranger than a monkey leapin' like a frog,
Frank the cat thought he was a dog.

1

Frank the cat would fetch the stick
to have a little fun.
The other cats said, "What's up with that?"
while lazin' in the sun.

Frank the cat would have none of that
and go racin' through the park.

Frank the cat thought he was a dog -
everybody thought it was so odd.
Stranger than a monkey leapin' like a frog,
Frank the cat thought he was a dog.
(Isn't that strange?)

Frank the cat was watchin' dogs
buryin' their bones.
Frank the cat thought that was cool,
and got one of his own.

6

While the cats were gettin' fat
lyin' 'round the house,
Frank the cat would have none of that -
he didn't like eating mouse... "BLECK" !!!

"CUZ"

Frank the cat thought he was a dog –
everybody thought it was so odd.
Stranger than a monkey leapin' like a frog,
Frank the cat thought he was a dog.
(Isn't that peculiar?)

Frank the cat had a boy who he liked to train
to take him out for a walk, even in the rain.

Frank the cat thought he was a dog -
everybody thought it was so odd.
Stranger than a monkey leapin' like a frog,
Frank the cat thought he was a
thought he was a
thought he was a
dog... "MEARK!"

FRANK

Frank

FRANK THE CAT

words and music by Angela Kelman and Allan Rodger

FRANK THE CAT - lyrics

Frank the cat thought he was a dog
Everybody thought it was so odd
Stranger than a monkey leapin' like a frog
Frank the cat, thought he was a dog

Frank the cat would fetch the stick to
have a little fun
The other cats said "what's up with that"
while lazin' in the sun
Frank the cat would have none of that and
go racin' through the park
When the kids called out his name, he let
out a "MEARK"
"CUZ"

Frank the cat thought he was a dog
Everybody thought it was so odd
Stranger than a monkey leapin' like a frog
Frank the cat, thought he was a dog
isn't that a little strange???

Frank the cat was watchin' dogs buryin'
their bones
Frank the cat thought that was cool and
got one of his own
While the cats were gettin' fat lyin' 'round
the house
Frank the cat would have none of that
He didn't like eating mouse... "BLECK!"
"Cuz"

Frank the cat thought he was a dog
Everybody thought it was so odd
Stranger than a monkey leapin' like a frog
Frank the cat thought he was a dog
(Isn't that peculiar?)

Frank the cat had a boy who he liked to train
To take him out for a walk even in the rain
The other cats just shook their heads and
laughed at man's best friend
But everyone loved Frank the cat
Who started this new trend
"Cuz"

Frank the cat thought he was a dog
Everybody thought it was so odd
Stranger than a monkey leapin' like a frog
Frank the cat thought he was a "dowg"
(A "New Yowk Dowg" even)

To all you kids listening to this song
Being different doesn't mean it's wrong
"Bark" like a dog "Meow" like a cat
If you mix 'em up nothin' wrong with that
"Cuz"

Frank the cat thought he was a dog
Everybody thought it was so odd
Stranger than a monkey leapin' like a frog
Frank the cat thought he was a
Thought he was a
Thought he was a dog..."Meark!"

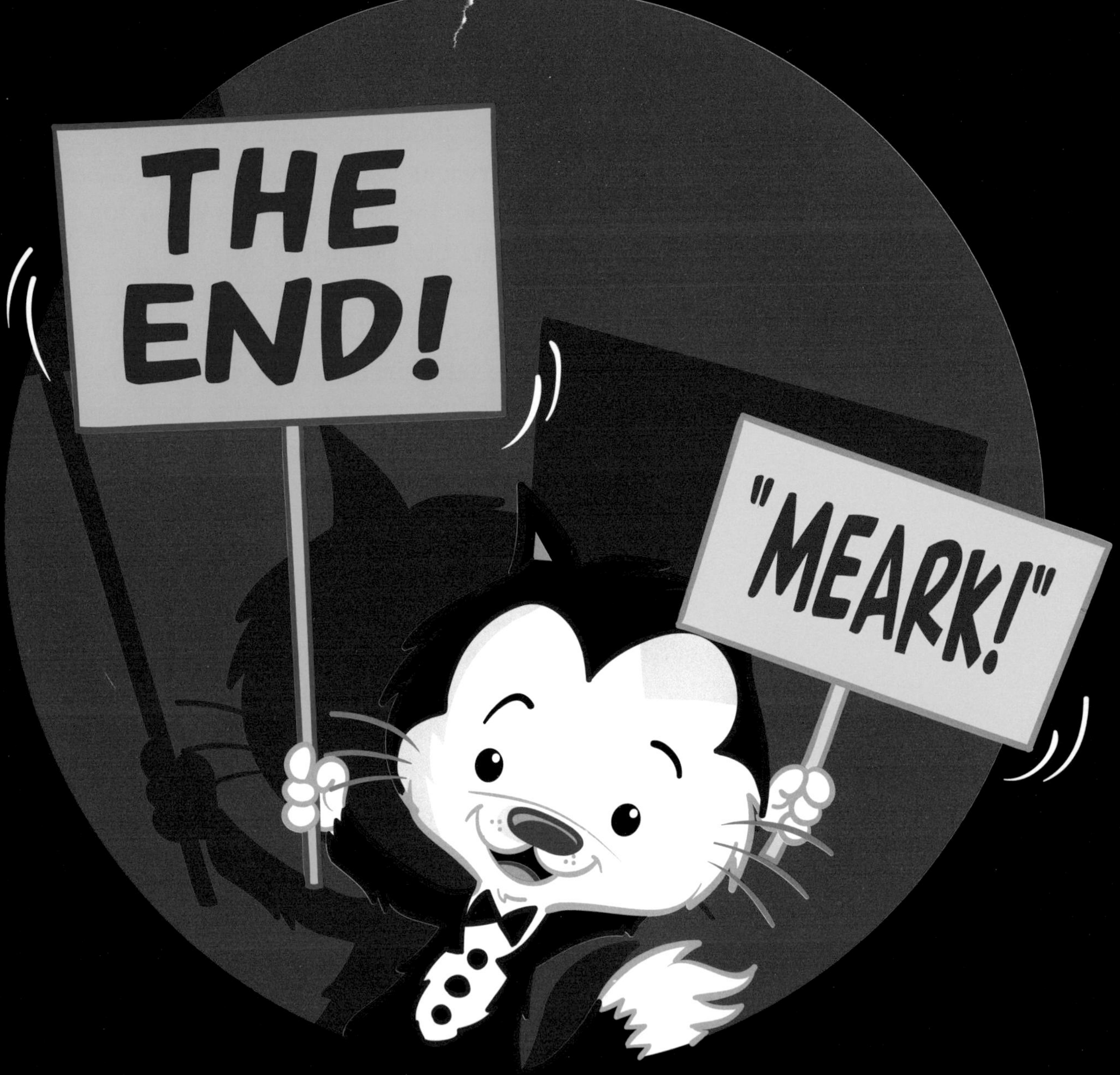
THE END!
"MEARK!"